P9-CAO-673

DATE DUE

JUN 16 2015		
OCT 26 2015		
APR 2 3 2016		
12/1/16		

JUN

GAYLORD   PRINTED IN U.S.A.

THE THREE PRINCESSES

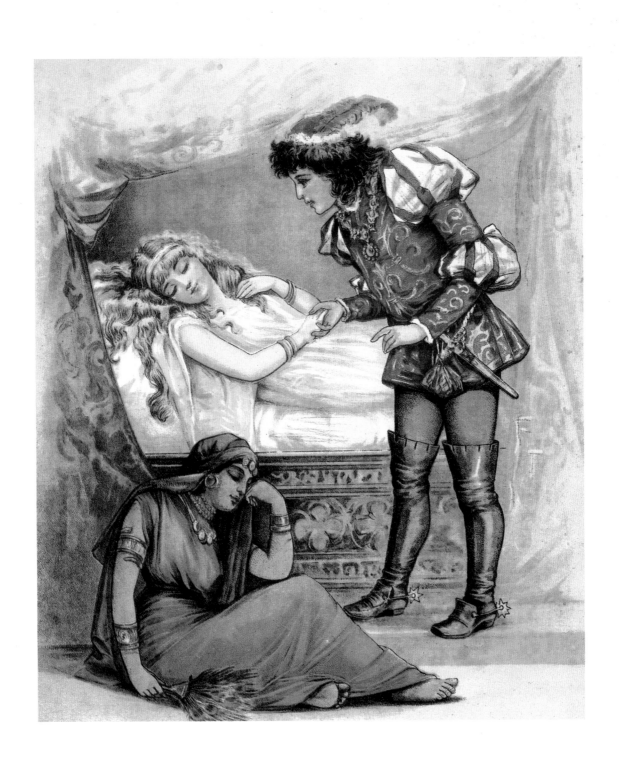

THE THREE PRINCESSES

CINDERELLA,
SLEEPING BEAUTY,
AND
SNOW WHITE

The Ultimate Illustrated Edition

Conceived, Compiled, and Arranged
by Cooper Edens

BANTAM BOOKS
NEW YORK • TORONTO • LONDON • SYDNEY • AUCKLAND

ACKNOWLEDGMENTS

The illustration by Eulalie is reprinted by permission of Platt & Munk, Publishers from *Stories Children Love* edited by Watty Piper, copyright 1927, copyright renewed © 1955 by Platt & Munk, Publishers. The illustrations by Bess Livings from *Snow White and the Seven Dwarfs*, copyright 1937, and the illustrations by Margaret Evans Price from *Once Upon a Time*, copyright 1921, are reprinted with the permission of Macmillan Publishing Co.

THE THREE PRINCESSES
A Bantam Book / October 1991

Library of Congress Cataloging-in-Publication Data

The three princesses: the ultimate illustrated edition / complied & arranged by
  Cooper Edens.
     p.   cm.
  Includes bibliographical references.
  Summary: Presents three fairy tales about princesses: Snow White, Sleeping
Beauty, and Cinderella. Author's notes present historical background on these
tales, which occur in many countries.
  ISBN 0-553-07368-0
  1. Fairy tales. [1. Fairy tales. 2. Folklore. 3. Princesses—Folklore.]
I. Edens, Cooper.
PZ8.T4119 1991
398.21--dc20
                                                        90-45294
                                                           CIP
                                                            AC
          Published simultaneously in the United States and Canada

PRINTED IN THE UNITED STATES OF AMERICA

0 9 8 7 6 5 4 3 2 1

Introduction

There is an abundance of folklore available to humankind. Each culture's account of these tales, indeed each individual retelling, is a combination of preexisting symbols which have appeared in various forms around the world. The stories which have survived are those which fuse these symbols most adroitly.

Gathering the stories of the three princesses, Cinderella, Sleeping Beauty, and Snow White, into one volume combines some of the most astonishing symbolism in all literature. From Cinderella's glass slipper and midnight warning to Sleeping Beauty's spindle and hundred-year spell to the living mirror and glass coffin in Snow White, we find evidence of our fascination with the arcane through the centuries.

But even these symbols are faint in comparison to what I believe to be the three princesses' common origin and shared purpose. The stories of three girls supernaturally involved in becoming princesses are, in fact, one and the same story—a story that clearly represents to us that evil absolutely cannot destroy what is real and good.

There is a romantic idea that folktales come from the people. They don't. Folktales come from teachers, shamans, and visionaries who translate what they see and hear into ritual forms. Other visionaries then reinvent these forms and breathe new life into them as time passes.

Such has been the destiny of the three princesses. Beginning with the oldest princess, Cinderella, over a thousand years ago in China, spreading with her sisters Sleeping Beauty and Snow White into thousands of different tellings around the world, these stories were graced by the master illustrators, Rackham, Dulac, Sowerby, Robinson, and eventually glorified on film by Walt Disney.

Now as we near the end of another century there is no argument: The three princesses are powerful, if not indomitable. They exist on their own, free from their creators, and rich in the promise to always exist and never have the virtue they symbolize transcended.

Cooper Edens

CONTENTS

CINDERELLA .... Page 5

SLEEPING BEAUTY .... Page 59

SNOW WHITE .... Page 105

CINDERELLA

by Charles Perrault
as refined by Mrs. Edgar Lucas
from the original English translation
of Robert Samber

PREFACE

Scholars have identified more than seven hundred versions of Cinderella. The earliest was recorded by a Chinese scholar in the ninth century. In this version the despised stepdaughter is helped by the bones of a pet fish. The wonderful garments she wears to the festival include a pair of gold shoes. The king searches for the beauty who can wear the exquisite shoes, finds and marries her, but before this time the cruel stepmother and her favored daughters are killed by flying rocks.

In a seventeenth-century Italian version the heroine plots to kill her stepmother. A tree dresses her for the ball. At the ball she drops a high heeled shoe, with the help of which the king finds her.

In Madame d'Aulnoy's *Finetta the Cinder Girl* (France, 1721) the heroine finds the key to a locked chest where she discovers the ball gown. The slipper she loses is made from red velvet, braided with pearls. After the king finds and marries her, they invite the two favored sisters to come and live at court.

In the Grimm version of Cinderella, *Aschenputtel* (1826) a little white bird provides the beautiful ball dress and golden slippers. The prince eventually obtains one of these slippers by coating the staircase of the ballroom with pitch. Aschenput-tel's cruel sister cuts off her big toes to make the shoe fit, and the prince is deceived, but on the way to her wedding two pigeons warn him of the deception. A second sister tries the same grotesque trick with similar results. The tattletale pigeons peck out the sisters' eyes while they are acting as bridesmaids.

A nineteenth-century Scottish version, *Rashin Coaties* uses a slain red calf to provide the heroine with her beautiful clothes and satin shoes. The mother cuts off a portion of her favored daughter's foot to make the shoe fit, but birds tell the prince, and the shoe jumps out of his pocket and onto the foot of the true beloved.

In this book we use an early English translation of the French version as told by Charles and Pierre Perrault in *Histoires ou Contes du Temps Passé*, published in Paris in 1697. This version seems to me to be the product of flawless judg-ment. It is recognizably the same basic story told in the other versions, but at every place where Perrault had to choose between sources he made the tasteful choice. For example, he was the first to recognize the beauty and delicacy of unstretchable glass slippers. The result is a beauti-fully balanced version of a powerful story.

THERE was once an honest gentleman who took for his second wife the proudest and most disagreeable lady in the whole country. She had two daughters exactly like herself. He himself had one little girl, who resembled her dead mother, the best woman in all the world. Scarcely had the second marriage taken place before the stepmother became jealous of the good qualities of the little girl, who was so great a contrast to her own two daughters. She gave her all the hard work of the house, compelling her to wash the floors and staircases, to dust the bedrooms, and to clean the grates. While her sisters occupied carpeted chambers hung with mirrors, where they could see themselves from head to foot, this poor little girl was sent to sleep in an attic, on an old straw mattress, with only one chair and not a looking-glass in the room.

She suffered all in silence, not daring to complain to her father, who was entirely ruled by his new wife. When her daily work was done she used to sit down in the chimney corner among the ashes, from which the two sisters gave her the nickname of "Cinderella." But Cinderella, however shabbily clad, was handsomer than they were, with all their fine clothes.

It happened that the king's son gave a series of balls, to which were invited all the rank and fashion of the city, and among the rest the two elder sisters. They were very proud and happy, and occupied their whole time in deciding what they should wear. This was a source of new trouble to Cinderella, whose duty it was to get up their fine linen and laces, and who never could please them, however much she tried.

They talked of nothing but their clothes.

"I," said the elder, "shall wear my velvet gown and my trimmings of English lace."

"And I," added the younger, "will have but my ordinary silk petticoat, but I shall adorn it with an upper skirt of flowered brocade, and shall put on my diamond tiara, which is a great deal finer than anything of yours."

Here the elder sister grew angry, and the dispute began to run so high that Cinderella, who was known to have excellent taste, was called upon to decide between them. She gave them the best advice she could, and gently and submissively offered to dress them herself, and especially to arrange their hair, an accomplishment in which she excelled many a noted coiffeur.

The important evening came, and she exercised all her skill in adorning the two young ladies. While she was combing out the elder's hair this ill-natured girl said sharply, "Cinderella, do you not wish you were going to the ball?"

"Ah, madam"—they obliged her always to say madam—"you are only mocking me; it is not my fortune to have any such pleasure."

"You are right; people would only laugh to see a little cinder-wench at a ball."

After this any other girl would have dressed the hair all awry, but Cinderella was good and made it perfectly even and smooth.

The sisters had scarcely eaten for two days and had broken a dozen stay-laces a day in trying to make themselves slender; but tonight they broke a dozen more, and lost their tempers over and over again before they had completed their toilette. When at last the happy moment arrived Cinderella followed them to the coach, and after it had whirled them away she sat down by the kitchen fire and cried.

Immediately her godmother, who was a fairy, appeared beside her. "What are you crying for, my little maid?"

"Oh, I wish—I wish—" Her sobs stopped her.
"You wish to go to the ball, isn't it so?"
Cinderella nodded.
"Well, then, be a good girl, and you shall go. First run into the garden and fetch me the largest pumpkin you can find."

Cinderella did not understand what this had to do with her going to the ball, but, being obedient and obliging, she went. Her godmother took the pumpkin and, having scooped out all its inside, struck it with her wand.

No sooner did the wand touch the pumpkin than it became a splendid gilt coach, lined with rose-colored satin.

"Now fetch me the mousetrap out of the pantry, my dear."

Cinderella brought it; it contained six of the fattest, sleekest mice.

The fairy lifted up the wire door, and as each mouse ran out she struck it and changed it into a beautiful white horse.

"But what shall I do for your coachman, Cinderella?"

Cinderella suggested that she had seen a large black rat in the rat trap, and he might do for want of better.

"You are right. Go and look again for him."

He was found, and the fairy made him into a most respectable coachman, with the finest whiskers imaginable.

24

She afterwards took six lizards from behind the pumpkin frame and changed them into six footmen, all in splendid livery, who immediately jumped up behind the carriage, as if they had been footmen all their days.

"Well, Cinderella, now you can go to the ball."

"What, in these clothes?" said Cinderella piteously, looking down on her ragged frock.

Her godmother laughed, and touched her also with the wand, at which her wretched, threadbare jacket became stiff with gold and sparkling with jewels, her woollen petticoat lengthened into a gown of sweeping satin, from underneath which peeped out her little feet, covered with silk stockings and the prettiest glass slippers in the world.

"Now, Cinderella, you may go; but remember, if you stay one instant after midnight your carriage will become a pumpkin, your coachman a rat, your horses mice, and your footmen lizards, while you yourself will be the little cinder-wench you were an hour ago."

Cinderella promised without fear, her heart was so full of joy.

When she arrived at the palace, the king's son, whom someone, probably the fairy, had told to await the coming of an uninvited princess whom nobody knew, was standing at the entrance, ready to receive her. He offered her his hand, and led her with the utmost courtesy through the assembled guests, who stood aside to let her pass, whispering to one another, "Oh, how beautiful she is!" It might have turned the head of anyone but poor Cinderella, who was so used to being despised, but she took it all as if it were something happening in a dream.

Her triumph was complete; even the old king said to the queen that never since Her Majesty's young days had he seen so charming a person. All the court ladies scanned her eagerly, clothes and all, and determined to have theirs made the next day of exactly the same pattern.

The king's son himself led her out to dance, and she danced so gracefully that he admired her more and more. Indeed, at supper, which was fortunately early, his admiration quite took away his appetite.

Cinderella herself sought out her sisters, placed herself beside them, and offered them all sorts of civil attentions. These, coming as they supposed from a stranger, and so magnificent a lady, almost overwhelmed them with delight.

While she was talking with them she heard the clock strike a quarter to twelve, and, making a courteous *adieu* to the royal family, she re-entered her carriage, escorted gallantly by the king's son, and arrived in safety at her own door.

There she found her godmother, who smiled approval, and of whom she begged permission to go to a second ball the following night, to which the queen had invited her.

While she was talking the two sisters were heard knocking at the gate, and the fairy godmother vanished, leaving Cinderella sitting in the chimney corner, rubbing her eyes and pretending to be very sleepy.

"Ah," cried the eldest sister spitefully, "it has been the most delightful ball, and there was present the most beautiful princess I ever saw, who was so exceedingly polite to us both."

"Was she?" said Cinderella indifferently. "And who might she be?"

"Nobody knows, though everybody would give their eyes to know, especially the king's son."

"Indeed!" replied Cinderella, a little more interested. "I should like to see her." Then she turned to the elder sister and said, "Miss Javotte, will you not let me go tomorrow, and lend me your yellow gown that you wear on Sundays?"

"What, lend my yellow gown to a cinder-wench! I am not so mad as that!"

Cinderella did not complain, for if her sister really had lent her the gown she would have been considerably embarrassed.

The next night came, and the two young ladies, richly dressed in different toilettes, went to the ball. Cinderella, more splendidly attired and more beautiful than ever, followed them shortly after. "Now, remember twelve o'clock" was her godmother's parting speech; and she thought she certainly should.

Millicent Sowerby

But the prince's attentions to her were even greater than on the first evening, and in the delight of listening to his pleasant conversation time slipped by unperceived. While she was sitting beside him in a lovely alcove and looking at the moon from under a bower of orange blossom she heard a clock strike the first stroke of twelve.

She started up and fled away as lightly as a deer.

Amazed, the prince followed but could not catch her. Indeed, he missed his lovely princess altogether, and only saw running out of the palace doors a little dirty lass whom he had never beheld before, and of whom he certainly would never have taken the least notice.

Cinderella arrived at home breathless and weary, ragged and cold, without carriage or footmen or coachman; the only remnant of her past magnificence being one of her little glass slippers; the other she had dropped in the ballroom as she ran away.

When the two sisters returned they were full of this strange adventure: how the beautiful lady had appeared at the ball more beautiful than ever, and enchanted everyone who looked at her; and how as the clock was striking twelve she had suddenly risen up and fled through the ballroom, disappearing no one knew how or where, and dropping one of her glass slippers behind her in her flight.

The king's son had remained inconsolable until he chanced to pick up the little glass slipper, which he carried away in his pocket and was seen to take out continually and look at affectionately, with the air of a man very much in love; in fact, from his behavior during the remainder of the evening all the court and the royal family were sure that he was desperately in love with the wearer of the little glass slipper.

Cinderella listened in silence, turning her face to the kitchen fire, and perhaps it was that which made her look so rosy; but nobody ever noticed or admired her at home, so it did not signify, and the next morning she went to her weary work again just as before.

A few days later the whole city was attracted by the sight of a herald going around with a little glass slipper in his hand, publishing, with a flourish of trumpets, that the king's son ordered this to be tried on the foot of every lady in the kingdom, and that he wished to marry the lady whom it fit best, or to whom it and the fellow slipper belonged. Princesses, duchesses, countesses, and simple gentlewomen all tried it on, but, being a fairy slipper, it did not fit anyone; and, besides, nobody could produce its fellow slipper, which lay all the time safely in the pocket of Cinderella's old woolen gown.

At last the herald came to the house of the two sisters, and though they well knew neither of themselves was the beautiful lady they made every attempt to get their clumsy feet into the glass slipper, but in vain.

"Let me try it on," said Cinderella from the chimney corner.

"What, you?" cried the others, bursting into shouts of laughter. But Cinderella only smiled and held out her hand.

Millicent Sowerby.

Her sisters could not prevent her, since the command was that every maiden in the city should try on the slipper, in order that no chance might be left untried, for the prince was nearly breaking his heart, and his father and mother were afraid that he would actually die for love of the beautiful unknown lady.

So the herald bade Cinderella to sit down on a three-legged stool in the kitchen, and he himself put the slipper on her pretty little foot. It fit exactly.

She then drew from her pocket the fellow slipper, which she also put on, and stood up. With the touch of the magic shoes all her dress was changed likewise. No longer was she the poor, despised cinder-wench, but the beautiful lady whom the king's son loved.

Her sisters recognized her at once. Filled with astonishment, mingled with no little alarm, they threw themselves at her feet, begging her pardon for all their former unkindness.

She raised and embraced them, telling them she forgave them with all her heart, and only hoped they would love her always. Then she departed with the herald to the king's palace, and told her whole story to His Majesty and the royal family. They were not in the least surprised, for everybody believed in fairies, and everybody longed to have a fairy godmother.

As for the young prince, he found her more lovely and lovable than ever and insisted upon marrying her immediately. Cinderella never went home again, but she sent for her two sisters and married them shortly after to two rich gentlemen of the court.

SLEEPING BEAUTY

SLEEPING BEAUTY

by Charles Perrault
as refined by Richard Marshall
and Cluer Dicey from the original
English translation
of Robert Samber

PREFACE

The earliest hint of the legend of Sleeping Beauty is the fourteenth-century Scandinavian *Volsunga Saga* in which Udin places Brynhild in a castle surrounded by a forest of flame and puts her into a timeless sleep to await a hero who could brave the flames and free her from the spell.

The fourteenth-century French romance *Peroeforest* includes a story called "Troylus and Zellandine." The little princess Zellandine is cursed by a minor goddess who is slighted at the birth celebration. Her curse, unlike that put upon Sleeping Beauty, is not announced, but many years later, when the princess is pierced while spinning, she falls into a trance. Up to this point the story is similar to ours, but it veers off in an ugly direction when the prince rapes the sleeping heroine.

Perrault's version, *La Belle au Bors Dormant* was published in 1696 and, because of his taste and literary skill, is the one that has prevailed. Curiously, the event we all remember when the prince kisses Sleeping Beauty back to life is a later addition. In Perrault the prince merely kneels at her side and she is wakened by the sense of his presence and love. The story published in this book differs from the Perrault in one important way: It omits the lengthy episode in which the prince's mother, an ogress, attempts to kill and eat the two children borne of her son and Sleeping Beauty, and then she finally tries to eat her daughter-in-law. In each of these attempts she is foiled, and finally she throws herself into a pot of vipers that she has prepared for her victims. I have rejected this not because it is gory, for this is typical in fairy tales, but because it seems to be tacked onto the end of a lovely story which has already been satisfactorily concluded.

ONG ago, in fairy times, there lived a king and
queen who were very happy, having nothing to complain of but the want of children to share their joy.
At last it pleased Providence to present them with
a daughter. At the birth of this princess there was great joy all
over the kingdom; and at the christening seven fairies were
asked to stand as godmothers, in the hope that each would
offer the little princess some gift, as was always done in those
days, by which means she would be adorned with every good
thing that could be thought of or wished for.

The christening being over, a grand feast was prepared to
entertain and thank the fairies. Before each of them was laid
a splendid dish, with a spoon, a knife, and a fork of richly
carved, pure gold. Just as they were going to sit down, in came
a very old fairy who had not been invited. The king ordered
a plate to be laid for her, but he could not give her such a case
of gold as the others had, because he had had only seven
made—one for each of the fairies. The aged fairy, thinking
that she was slighted, muttered many threats, which were
overheard by one of the fairies who sat beside her. Judging that
the old fairy might give the little princess some fatal gifts, the
young fairy hid herself behind the hangings of the room, that
she might speak last and undo as much as possible the evil
which the old fairy might intend.

Meanwhile the fairies began to bestow their gifts on the princess. The youngest gave her great beauty; another gave her wit; and so on with the others until the old fairy's turn came. She went forward, and with a shaking head, more from spite than from age, she said that the princess would have her hand pierced with a spindle, and that she would die of the wound. These awful words made the whole company tremble.

At this instant the young fairy came out from behind the curtains and spoke these words:

"Be comforted, O king and queen, and be assured that your daughter shall not die of this evil. It is true that I have not power to undo what my elder has done. The princess shall indeed pierce her hand with a spindle; but instead of dying, she shall only fall into a deep sleep, which shall last one hundred years, at the end of which a king's son will come and awaken her."

Yet the king, to turn aside the evil spoken by the old fairy, sent forth a royal order whereby every person was forbidden, on pain of death, to spin with a distaff or spindle, or even to keep them in their houses.

About fifteen years later, when the king and queen were gone on a visit to one of their summer palaces, the young princess, to amuse herself, went over the rooms of the palace, and, in the gaiety of youth, climbed one of the turrets, where, in a little garret, she found an old woman spinning with the distaff. This good woman had never heard of the king's order against the spindle.

"What are you doing, Goody?" asked the princess. "I am spinning, my pretty lady," replied the old woman, not knowing who she was. "Oh, that is very pretty!" said the princess, "how do you do it? Give it to me, that I may try."

The old woman, to please the lady, granted her request. She had no sooner taken it into her hand than, being somewhat hasty and careless, the spindle pierced her hand, and she fell down in a swoon.

The good old woman became alarmed and, not knowing what to do, called aloud for help. A number of servants flocked around the princess, trying every means to restore her, but all to no purpose.

And when the king returned, he remembered the prediction of the fairies, and judging very well that this must necessarily come to pass since the fairies had said it, he had the princess carried into the finest apartment in the palace, and laid upon a bed all embroidered with gold and silver. One would have taken her for a little angel, she was so very beautiful; for her swooning away had not diminished one bit of her complexion: her cheeks were carnation, and her lips like coral. She had only her eyes shut, but they heard her breathe softly, which satisfied them that she was not dead. The king commanded that they should not disturb her, but let her sleep quietly till her hour of awakening was come.

The good fairy, who had promised to save her life by causing her to sleep for a hundred years, was in the kingdom of Matakin, twelve thousand leagues off, when this accident befell the princess; but she was instantly informed of it by a dwarf who had boots with which he could tread over many leagues of ground at a stride.

The fairy left the kingdom at once and arrived at the palace about an hour later in a chariot drawn by dragons.

The king handed her out of the chariot, and she approved of everything he had done; but as she had great foresight, she thought that when the princess should awake, she might be puzzled what to do on finding herself alone in this large old palace. She therefore touched with her wand all the ladies-in-waiting, gentlemen—in short, every person in the palace except the king and queen; she likewise touched all the horses and all the dogs down to the little spaniel that lay beside her on the bed.

No sooner had she done so than they all fell into a sound sleep that was to last till their mistress should awake, that they might be ready to wait upon her. All this was done in a moment, fairies never being long in doing their spiriting.

The king and queen, having kissed their child without waking her, left the palace, and sent forth an order forbidding anyone to come near the spot. This, however, was needless, for in less than a quarter of an hour there sprang up all around the park such a vast number of trees, great and small bushes, briers and brambles, twined one within the other, that neither man nor beast could pass through. Nothing could be seen but the tops of the towers of the palace, and even these only from a good way off. Indeed the fairy had given a wonderful example of her art, in order that the princess, while she remained sleeping, might be quite secure from prying eyes.

One
hundred
years
after

At the end of one hundred years, the son of the king who then reigned (but not of the same family as the sleeping princess) being out hunting on that side of the country, asked what these towers were, the tops of which he saw in the midst of a great thick wood. Everyone answered according as he had heard.

Some said it was an old ruinous castle haunted by spirits; others, that it was a place of meeting for all the witches in the land; while the most common opinion was that an ogre lived there who was in the habit of stealing all the little children he could, that he might eat them up at his leisure without anybody being able to follow him, as he himself only had the power to pass through the wood.

The prince did not know what to make of these different accounts, when an aged countryman said, "May it please Your Highness, it is about fifty years since I heard my father tell what his father had told him—that there was then in this castle a princess, the most beautiful that was ever seen; that she must sleep there for a hundred years, and would be awakened by a king's son whose bride she would become."

The young prince felt much excited at these words and, with the hope of being himself the hero who was to end the long fairy-sleep, resolved that moment to look into it and find out how far the story might prove true.

Scarcely had he advanced towards the wood when all the great trees, the bushes and brambles, gave way of their own accord to allow him to pass through.

He came into a large outer courtyard, where everything he saw might have frightened anyone less brave than himself. There reigned over all a frightful silence.

The image of death was everywhere present, for there was nothing to be seen but the bodies of men and animals, all seeming to be dead.

Hurrying along the corridor

He, however, very well knew, by the jolly, rosy faces of the porters, that they were only asleep with their goblets in their hands, plainly showing they all had fallen asleep in their cups. He then crossed a court paved with marble, went upstairs, and entered the guard chamber, where the guards were standing in their ranks with their guns upon their shoulders and snoring loudly.

After that he went through several rooms full of ladies and gentlemen-in-waiting, some standing and others sitting, but all fast asleep.

At last he entered a chamber all gilt with gold. Here he saw
upon a splendid bed, the finest sight that ever he beheld—

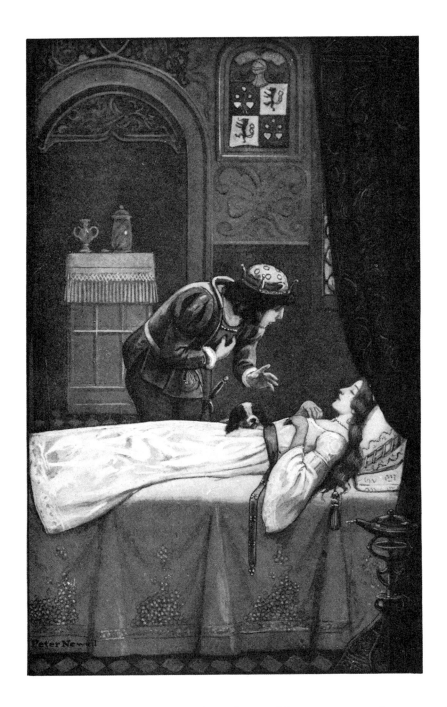

a princess who seemed to be about fifteen years of age, and whose rare beauty had in it something divine.

He went near with fear and trembling, and could not keep
from bending his knee before her.

Now the trance was at an end. The princess awoke and
looked on him with eyes more tender than the first view would
seem to admit of. "Is it you, my prince? How long I've been
waiting for you!" The prince, charmed with these words and
the manner in which they were spoken, assured her that he
loved her far better than himself.

Their meeting was so quiet that indeed they wept more than they talked. He was more at a loss for words than she was, and little wonder, as she had had time to think on what to say to him; for it was very probable, though the history mentions nothing of it, that the good fairy during so long a sleep had given her pleasant dreams. In short, they talked for about four hours together, and yet said not half of what they had to say.

In the meantime, the people of the palace, having awoke at the same time as the princess, each began to perform the duties of his or her office; and as they were not all in love like their mistress, but were rather ready to die with hunger, the lady-in-waiting grew very impatient and told the princess that supper was served. The prince helped the princess to rise; for she was already dressed in splendid robes, though His Royal Highness did not tell her that her clothes were cut on the pattern of those of his great-grandmother, which were long out of fashion. However, she looked no less beautiful than if her dress had been more modern.

They went into the great hall of looking-glasses, where they supped to the sound of delightful music.

With fiddles and spinet, tunes a century old were played. After supper the chaplain joined the happy pair in wedlock.

The next day they left the old castle and returned to court, where the king was delighted to welcome back the prince with his lovely bride, who was thenceforth known, both by her own people and by those who handed down the story to us, as the "Sleeping Beauty of the Wood."

SNOW WHITE

Snow-white

by Jacob and Wilhelm Grimm
as told to them by
Jannette and Amalie Hassenpflug
Translation by D. M. M. Craik

PREFACE

Snow White was collected by the Grimm brothers from two sisters, Jannette and Amalie Hassenpflug, in approximately 1823. The story, in roughly the same form, has been found in Ireland, Africa, and the Middle East. Like most folktales, the story is a combination of preexisting themes and ideas found throughout the world.

The theme of a stepmother's jealousy of a beautiful stepdaughter is universal. The idea of this situation being exacerbated by a talking mirror is similar to a Somali tale in which a king is warned about rebellious subjects by a talking mirror, and a Tuscan tale in which a maiden continually checks on the state of her beauty with her speaking mirror. The compassionate executioner who cannot obey his instructions is widespread. The old English ballad *The Babes in the Wood* is one of the best known embodiments of this situation. The idea of dwarfs living alone and making their living by mining is very like the situation described in a thirteenth-century German poem in which it is said that God created the dwarfs "because the mountains lay waste and useless, and valuable stores of silver and gold, with gems and pearls, were concealed in them. Therefore God made the dwarfs right wise and crafty; they could distinguish good and bad, and to what use all things could be applied." The glass coffin occurs in another Grimm story, *The Glass Coffin* and in the Italian book *The Pentamerone*, in which a seven-year-old girl, apparently dead from a witch's curse, is buried. In this story the casket gradually enlarges as the girl grows into a woman.

To point out that the elements from which Snow White is constructed are part of an ancient and universal body of narrative devices should in no way detract from its merit, for storytellers make their stories from what lies at hand in the same way composers build with notes and phrases. In the case of Snow White the result is unforgettable.

ONCE upon a time, in the middle of winter, when the flakes of snow fell like feathers from the sky, a queen sat at a window set in an ebony frame and sewed. While she was sewing and watching the snow fall, she pricked her finger with her needle, and three drops of blood dropped on the snow. And because the crimson looked so beautiful on the white snow, she thought, "Oh that I had a child as white as snow, as red as blood, and as black as the wood of this ebony frame!"

Soon afterwards she had a little daughter, who was as white as snow, as red as blood, and had hair as black as ebony. She was named Snow White. And when the child was born, the queen died.

After a year had gone by, the king took another wife. She was a handsome lady, but proud and haughty, and could not endure that anyone should surpass her in beauty. She had a wonderful mirror, and whenever she walked up to it and looked at herself in it, she said:

"Little glass upon the wall,
    Who is fairest among us all?"

Then the mirror replied:

"Lady queen, so grand and tall,
    Thou art the fairest of them all."

And she was satisfied, for she knew the mirror always told the truth. But Snow White grew ever taller and fairer, and at seven years old was beautiful as the day, and more beautiful than the queen herself. So once, when the queen asked of her mirror:

"Little glass upon the wall,
    Who is fairest among us all?"

It answered:

"Lady queen, you are grand and tall,
    But Snow White is fairest of you all."

Then the queen was startled, and turned yellow and green with envy. From that hour she so hated Snow White that she burned with secret wrath whenever she saw the maiden. Pride and envy grew apace like weeds in her heart, till she had no rest day or night.

113

So she called a huntsman and said, "Take the child out in the forest, for I will endure her no longer in my sight. Kill her and bring me her heart as a token that you have done it."

The huntsman obeyed and led the child away; but when he had drawn his hunting knife, and was about to pierce Snow White's innocent heart, she began to weep, and said, "Ah! dear huntsman, spare my life, and I will run deep into the wild forest and never more come home."

The huntsman took pity on her because she looked so lovely, and said, "Run away then, poor child!" The wild beasts will soon make an end of thee, he thought; but it seemed as if a stone had been rolled from his heart because he had avoided taking her life; and as a little bear came by just then, he killed it, took out its heart, and carried it as a token to the queen. She made the cook dress it with salt, and then the wicked woman ate it, and thought she had eaten Snow White's heart.

The poor child was now all alone in the great forest, and she felt frightened as she looked at all the leafy trees, and knew not what to do. So she began to run, and ran over the sharp stones, and through the thorns; and the wild beasts passed close to her, but did her no harm. She ran as long as her feet could carry her, and when evening closed in, she saw a little house, and went into it to rest herself.

Everything in the house was very small, but I cannot tell you how pretty and clean it was.

There stood a little table, covered with a white tablecloth, on which were seven little plates (each little plate with its own little spoon)—also seven little knives and forks, and seven little cups. Around the walls stood seven little beds close together, with sheets as white as snow. Snow White, being so hungry and thirsty, ate a little of the vegetables and bread on each plate, and drank a drop of wine from every cup, for she did not like to empty one entirely.

Then, being very tired, she laid herself down on one of the beds, but could not make herself comfortable, for one was too long, and another too short. The seventh, luckily, was just right; so there she stayed, said her prayers, and fell asleep.

When it had grown quite dark, home came the masters of the house, seven dwarfs, who delved and mined for iron among the mountains. They lighted their seven candles, and as soon as there was a light in the kitchen, they saw that someone had been there, for it was not quite so orderly as they had left it.

The first said, "Who has been sitting on my stool?"
The second, "Who has eaten off my plate?"
The third, "Who has taken part of my loaf?"
The fourth, "Who has touched my vegetables?"
The fifth, "Who has used my fork?"
The sixth, "Who has cut with my knife?"
The seventh, "Who has drunk out of my little cup?"

Then the first dwarf looked about and saw that there was a slight hollow in his bed, so he asked, "Who has been lying in my little bed?"

The others came running, and each called out, "Someone has also been lying in my bed."

But the seventh, when he looked at his bed, saw Snow White there, fast asleep. He called the others, who flocked around with cries of surprise, fetched their candles, and cast the light on Snow White.

"Oh, heaven!" they cried, "what a lovely child!" and were
so pleased that they would not wake her, but let her sleep on
in the little bed. The seventh dwarf slept with all his compan-
ions in turn, an hour with each, and so they spent the night.

When it was morning, Snow White woke up and was
frightened when she saw the seven dwarfs. They were friendly,
however, and inquired her name.

126

"Snow White," answered she.

"How have you found your way to our house?" asked the dwarfs.

So she told them how her stepmother had tried to kill her, how the huntsman had spared her life, and how she had run the whole day through, till at last she had found their little house.

Then the dwarfs said, "If thou wilt keep our house, cook, make our beds, wash, sew and knit, and make all neat and clean, thou canst stay with us, and shalt want for nothing."

"I will, right willingly," said Snow White.

So she dwelt with them, and kept their house in order.
For a time they knew great happiness.

Every morning they went out among the mountains to seek iron and gold, and came home ready for supper in the evening.

The maiden being left alone all day long, the good dwarfs warned her, saying, "Beware of thy wicked stepmother, who will soon find out that thou art here; take care that thou lettest nobody in."

The queen, however, after having, as she thought, eaten Snow White's heart, had no doubt that she was again the first and fairest woman in the world; so she walked up to her mirror and said:

"Little glass upon the wall,
 Who is fairest among us all?"

The mirror replied:

"Lady queen, so grand and tall,
 Here, you are fairest of them all;
 But over the hills, with the seven dwarfs old,
 Lives Snow White, fairer a hundredfold."

She trembled, knowing the mirror never told a falsehood; she felt sure that the huntsman had deceived her, and that Snow White was still alive. She pondered once more, late and early, early and late, how best to kill Snow White; for envy gave her no rest, day or night, while she herself was not the fairest lady in the land.

When she had planned what to do, she painted her face,
dressed herself like an old peddler woman, and altered her
appearance so much that no one could have known her. In this
disguise she went over the seven hills to where the seven
dwarfs dwelt, knocked at the door, and cried, "Good wares,
cheap! Very cheap!"

Snow White looked out of the window and cried, "Good
morning, good woman. What have you to sell?"

"Good wares, smart wares," answered the queen, "bodice
laces of all colors"; and drew out one which was woven of col-
ored silk.

"I may surely let this honest dame in!" thought Snow
White; so she unfastened the door, and bought for herself the
pretty lace.

135

"Child," said the old woman, "what a figure thou art! Let me lace thee for once properly." Snow White feared no harm, so stepped in front of her, and allowed her bodice to be fastened up with the new lace.

But the old woman laced so quick and laced so tight that Snow White's breath was stopped, and she fell down as if dead. "Now I am fairest at last," said the old woman to herself, and sped away.

The seven dwarfs came home soon after, at eventide, but how alarmed they were to find their poor Snow White lifeless on the ground! They lifted her up into bed and, seeing that she was laced too tightly, cut the lace of her bodice; she began to breathe faintly, and slowly returned to life. When the dwarfs heard what had happened, they said, "The old peddler woman was none other than the wicked queen. Be careful of thyself, and open the door to no one if we are not at home."

The cruel stepmother walked up to her mirror when she
reached home and said:

> "Little glass upon the wall,
>   Who is fairest among us all?"

To which it answered, as usual:

> "Lady queen, so grand and tall,
> Here, you are fairest of them all;
> But over the hills, with the seven dwarfs old,
> Lives Snow White, fairer a hundredfold."

When she heard this, she was so alarmed that all the blood rushed to her heart, for she saw plainly that Show White was still alive.

"This time," said she, "I will think of some means that shall destroy her utterly," and with the help of witchcraft, in which she was skillful, she made a poisoned comb. Then she changed her dress and took the shape of another old woman.

Again she crossed the seven hills to the home of the seven dwarfs, knocked at the door, and cried, "Good wares, very cheap!"

Snow White looked out and said, "Go away—I dare let no one in."

"You may surely be allowed to look!" answered the old woman, and she drew out the poisoned comb and held it up. The girl was so pleased with it that she let herself be cajoled, and opened the door.

When the bargain was struck, the dame said, "Now let me dress your hair properly for once." Poor Snow White took no heed, and let the old woman begin; but the comb had scarcely touched her hair before the poison worked, and she fell down senseless.

"Paragon of beauty!" said the wicked woman, "all is over with thee now," and went away.

Luckily, it was near evening, and the seven dwarfs soon came home. When they found Snow White lifeless on the ground, they at once distrusted her stepmother. They searched, and found the poisoned comb; and as soon as they had drawn it out, Snow White came to herself, and told them what had happened. Again they warned her to be careful, and open the door to no one.

The queen placed herself before the mirror at home and said:

> "Little glass upon the wall,
> Who is fairest among us all?"

But it again answered:

> "Lady queen, so grand and tall,
> Here, you are fairest of them all;
> But over the hills, with the seven dwarfs old,
> Lives Snow White, fairer a hundredfold."

When she heard the mirror speak thus, she quivered with rage. "Snow White shall die," she cried, "if it costs my own life!"

Then she went to a secret and lonely chamber, where no one ever disturbed her, and compounded an apple of deadly poison. Ripe and rosy-cheeked, it was so beautiful to look upon that all who saw it longed for it; but it brought death to any who should eat it. When the apple was ready, she painted her face, disguised herself as a peasant woman, and journeyed over the seven hills to where the seven dwarfs dwelt.

At the sound of the knock, Snow White put her head out of the window and said, "I cannot open the door to anybody, for the seven dwarfs have forbidden me to do so."

"Very well," replied the peasant woman; "I only want to be rid of my apples. Here I will give you one of them!"

"No!" said Snow White, "I dare not take it."

"Art thou afraid of being poisoned?" asked the old woman. "Look here; I will cut the apple in two, and you shall eat the rosy side, and I the white."

Now the fruit was so cunningly made, that only the rosy side was poisoned. Snow White longed for the pretty apple; and when she saw the peasant woman eating it, she could resist no longer, but stretched out her hand and took the poisoned half. She had scarcely tasted it when she fell lifeless to the ground.

The queen, laughing loudly, watched her with a barbarous look and cried, "O thou who art white as snow, red as blood, and black as ebony, the seven dwarfs cannot awaken thee this time!"

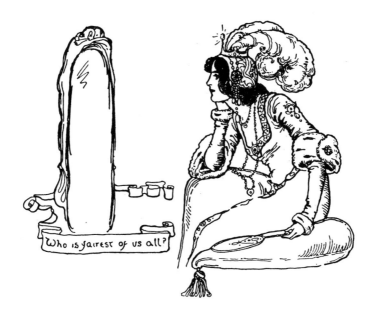

And when she asked the mirror at home:

> "Little glass upon the wall,
>   Who is fairest among us all?"

The mirror at last replied:

> "Lady queen, so grand and tall,
>   You are fairest of them all."

So her envious heart had as much repose as an envious heart can ever know.

When the dwarfs came home in the evening, they found
Snow White lying breathless and motionless on the ground.
They lifted her up, searched whether she had anything poison-
ous about her, unlaced her, combed her hair, washed her with
water and wine; but all was useless, for they could not bring
the darling back to life. They laid her on a bier, and all the
seven placed themselves around it, and mourned for her three
long days.

Then they would have buried her, but that she still looked so fresh and lifelike and had such lovely rosy cheeks. "We cannot lower her into the dark earth," they said; and they caused a transparent coffin of glass to be made, so that she could be seen on all sides, and laid her in it, writing her name outside in letters of gold, which told that she was the daughter of a king.

Then they placed the coffin on the mountain above, and one of them always stayed by it and guarded it. But there was little need to guard it, for even the wild animals came and mourned for Snow White. The birds likewise—first an owl, and then a raven, and afterwards a dove.

Long, long years did Snow White lie in her coffin unchanged, looking as though asleep, for she was still white as snow, red as blood, and her hair was black as ebony.

At last the son of a king chanced to wander into the forest, and came to the dwarfs' house for a night's shelter. He saw the coffin on the mountain with the beautiful Snow White in it, and read what was written there in letters of gold. Then he said to the dwarfs, "Let me have the coffin! I will give you whatever you like to ask for it."

But the dwarfs answered, "We would not part with it for all the gold in the world."

He said again, "Yet give it me; for I cannot live without seeing Snow White, and though she is dead, I will prize and honor her as my beloved."

Then the good dwarfs took pity on him and gave him the coffin.

The prince had it borne away by his servants. They happened to stumble over a bush, and the shock forced the bit of poisoned apple which Snow White had tasted out of her throat. Immediately she opened her eyes, raised the coffin lid, and sat up alive once more. "Oh, heaven!" cried she, "where am I?"

The prince answered joyfully, "Thou art with me," and told her what had happened, saying, "I love thee more dearly than anything else in the world. Come with me to my father's castle and be my wife."

Snow White, well pleased, went with him, and they were married with much state and grandeur.

The wicked stepmother was invited to the feast. Richly dressed, she stood before the mirror and asked of it:

"Little glass upon the wall,
   Who is fairest among us all?"

The mirror answered:

"Lady queen, so grand and tall,
   Here, you are fairest of them all;
   But the young queen over the mountains old,
   Is fairer than you a thousandfold."

162

The evil-hearted woman uttered a curse and could scarcely endure her anguish. She first resolved not to attend the wedding, but curiosity would not allow her to rest. She determined to travel and see who that young queen could be, who was the most beautiful in all the world. When she came and found that it was Snow White alive again, she stood petrified with terror and despair. Then two iron shoes, heated burning hot, were drawn out of the fire with a pair of tongs and laid before her feet. She was asked either to put them on, and to go and dance at Snow White's wedding—or to leave and nevermore be seen.

List of Illustrators

Listed in bibliographic form with illustrators' names in boldface.

Front cover: LEFT. **Anonymous.** *My Nursery Tale Book.* New York: E. P. Dutton and Co.; London: Ernest Nister, n.d.

CENTER. **Anonymous.** *My Nursery Tale Book.* New York: E. P. Dutton and Co.; London: Ernest Nister, n.d.

RIGHT. **Vogel, Herm.** *Kinder und Hausmärchen,* by Jacob and Wilhelm Grimm. Munich: Braun and Schneider, n.d.

Frontispiece: **Anonymous.** *The Nursery Picture Book.* London: Raphael Tuck and Sons, Ltd., n.d.

Copyright page: **Harbour, Jennie.** *My Book of Favourite Fairy Tales.* Edited by Capt. Eric Vredenburg, London: Raphael Tuck and Sons, Ltd.; Philadelphia: David McKay Company, n.d.

Page 2.   **Offerdinger, C.** *Märchenbuch.* Stuttgart: Wilhelm Effenberger, n.d.

3.   **Eulalie.** *Stories Children Love.* Edited by Watty Piper. New York: The Platt & Munk Co. Inc., 1927.

6.   **Bowley, A. L.** *Old Fairy Tales.* Edited by Capt. Eric Vredenburg, et al. London: Raphael Tuck and Sons, Ltd., n.d.

7.   **Anonymous.** *The Ideal Fairy Tales,* n.d.

8.   **Anonymous.** *Favourite Tales for the Nursery.* London: Thomas Nelson and Sons, 1894.

9.   **Anonymous.** *The Ideal Fairy Tales,* n.d.

10.   **Attwell, Mabel Lucie.** *The Fairy Book.* London: Thomas Nelson and Sons, Ltd., n.d.

11.   **Anonymous.** *Cinderella.* London: J. M. Dent, 1904.

12.   **Sowerby, Millicent.** *Cinderella.* Retold by Githa Sowerby. London: Henry, Frowde, Hodder and Stoughton, n.d.

13.   **Menerheim, Paul.** *Kinder und Hausmärchen,* by Jacob and Wilhelm Grimm. Gütersloh: C. Bertelsmann, 1895.

14.   **Hassall, John.** *The Old Nursery Stories and Rhymes.* Blackie and Son, Ltd., n.d.

15.   **Folkard, Charles.** *Grimm's Fairy Tales.* London: Adam and Charles Black, 1911.

16.   **Anonymous.** *The Ideal Fairy Tales,* n.d.

17.   **Smith, Jessie Willcox.** *A Child's Book of Stories.* Edited by Penrhyn W. Coussens. Duffield and Co., 1919.

18.   **Woodroffe, Paul.** *Nursery Tales,* by Amy Steedman. London: T. C. and E. C. Jack.; New York: E. P. Dutton and Co., n.d.

19.   **Anonymous.** *My Nursery Tale Book.* New York: E. P. Dutton and Co.; London: Ernest Nister, n.d.

20.   **Sowerby, Millicent.** *Cinderella.* Retold by Githa Sowerby. London: Henry, Frowde, Hodder and Stoughton, n.d.

21.   **Lawson, John.** *There Was Once!,* by Mrs. Oscar Wilde. London: Ernest Nister, n.d.

22.   **Doré, Gustave.** *Fairy Tales Told Again.* London: Cassell, Petter, and Galpin, n.d.

23. **Price, Margaret Evans.** *The Real Picture Book.* Edited by Katherine Lee Bates. New York: Rand McNally and Co., 1929.
24. **Anonymous.** *The Ideal Fairy Tales,* n.d.
25. **Margetson, W. H.** *The Old Fairy Tales.* New York: Sully and Kleinteich, n.d.
26. **Rackham, Arthur.** *Cinderella.* Retold by C. S. Evans. London: William Heinemann; Philadelphia: J. B. Lippincott Co., 1919.
27. **Anonymous.** *Les Contes du Foyer.* Paris: Imagerie D'Èpinal, n.d.
28. **Anonymous.** *Cinderella.* Edinburgh, n.d.
29. **Cole, Herbert.** *Fairy Gold.* Edited by Ernest Rhys. London: J. M. Dent and Co.; New York: E. P. Dutton and Co., 1906.
30. TOP: **Anonymous.** *There Was Once.* By Mrs. Oscar Wilde. London: Ernest Nister, n.d.
    BOTTOM: **Rackham, Arthur.** *The Arthur Rackham Fairy Book.* Edited by Arthur Rackham. Philadelphia: J. B. Lippincott Co., n.d.
31. **Dulac, Edmund.** *The Sleeping Beauty and Other Fairy Tales.* Retold by Sir Arthur Quiller-Couch. New York: Hodder and Stoughton, n.d.
32. **Anonymous.** *Les Contes du Foyer.* Paris: Imagerie D'Èpinal, n.d.
33. **Anonymous.** Cinderella. London: J. M. Dent, n.d.
34. **Harbour, Jennie.** *My Book of Favourite Fairy Tales.* Edited by Capt. Eric Vredenburg. London: Raphael Tuck and Sons, Ltd.; Philadelphia: David McKay Co., n.d.
35. **Lee, Ella Dolbear.** *Fifty Famous Fairy Tales.* Retold by Rosemary Kingston. Chicago: Whitman Publishing Co., 1917.
36. **Vogel, Herm.** *Kinder und Hausmärchen,* by Jacob and Wilhelm Grimm. Munich: Braun and Schneider, n.d.
37. **Hassell, John.** *The Old Nursery Stories and Rhymes.* Blackie and Son, Ltd., n.d.
38. **Gunston, W.** *Cinderella.* London: Frederick Warne and Co., c. 1876.
39. **Robinson, Charles.** *The Big Book of Fairy Tales.* Edited by Walter Jerrold. New York: H. M. Caldwell Co.; London: Blackie and Son, Ltd., n.d.
40. **Sowerby, Millicent.** *Cinderella.* Retold by Githa Sowerby. London: Henry, Frowde, Hodder and Stoughton, n.d.
41. **Harbour, Jennie.** *My Book of Favourite Fairy Tales.* Edited by Capt. Eric Vredenburg. London: Raphael Tuck and Sons, Ltd.; Philadelphia: David McKay Co., n.d.
42. **Tarrant, Margaret.** *Favourite Fairy Tales.* London: Ward, Lock and Co. Ltd., n.d.
43. **Offerdinger, C.** *Märchenbuch.* Stuttgart: Wilhelm Effenberger, n.d.

44. **Appleton, Honor.** *A Treasury of Tales For Little Folks.* Edited by Marjory Bruce. London: George G. Harrap and Co. Ltd., 1927.

45. **Crane, Walter.** *Cinderella.* London: Edmund Evans, 1873.

46. **Dulac, Edmund.** *The Sleeping Beauty and Other Fairy Tales.* Retold by Sir Arthur Quiller-Couch. New York: Hodder and Stoughton, n.d.

47. **Anonymous.** *The Ideal Fairy Tales,* n.d.

48. **Goble, Warwick.** *The Fairy Book.* London: Macmillan and Co. Ltd., 1913.

49. **Anonymous.** *The Ideal Fairy Tales,* n.d.

50. **Hassall, John.** *The Old Nursery Stories and Rhymes.* Blackie and Son, Ltd., n.d.

51. **Mack, Lizzie.** *A Christmas Tree Fairy,* by Robert Ellice Mack. New York: E. P. Dutton and Co., n.d.

52. **Robinson, Charles.** *The Big Book of Fairy Tales.* Edited by Walter Jerrold. New York: H. M. Caldwell Co.; London: Blackie and Son, Ltd., n.d.

53. **Sowerby, Millicent.** *Cinderella.* Retold by Githa Sowerby. London: Henry, Frowde, Hodder and Stoughton, n.d.

54. **Anonymous.** *The Nursery Picture Book.* London: Raphael Tuck and Sons, Ltd., n.d

55. **Newell, Peter.** *Favorite Fairy Tales.* New York: Harper and Brothers Publishers, 1907.

56. **Anonymous.** *The Story Teller.* Boston: Hall and Locke, 1902.

57. **Vogel, Herm.** *Kinder und Hausmärchen,* by Jacob and Wilhelm Grimm. Munich: Braun and Schneider, n.d.

60. **Appleton, Honor.** *Perrault's Fairy Tales.* Translated by S. R. Littlewood. London: Herbert and Daniel; Boston: Dana Estes and Co., n.d.

61. **Anonymous.** *The Ideal Fairy Tales,* n.d.

62. **Crane, Walter.** *Household Stories by the Brothers Grimm.* Translated by Lucy Crane. London: Macmillan and Co., 1886.

63. **Sowerby, Millicent.** *Grimm's Fairy Tales.* Retold by Githa Sowerby. London: Grant Richards, 1909.

64. **Tarrant, Margaret.** *Favourite Fairy Tales.* London: Ward, Lock and Co. Ltd., n.d.

65. **Anonymous.** *Favourite Stories for the Nursery.* London: Thomas Nelson and Sons, Ltd., 1891.

66. **Anonymous.** *The Ideal Fairy Tales,* n.d.

67. **Anonymous.** *The Ideal Fairy Tales,* n.d.

68. **Dulac, Edmund.** *The Sleeping Beauty and Other Fairy Tales.* Retold by Sir Arthur Quiller-Couch. New York: Hodder and Stoughton, n.d.

69. **Anonymous.** *The Nursery Picture Book.* London: Raphael Tuck

and Sons, Ltd., n.d.

70. **Richard Doyle.** *The Sleeping Beauty,* by Richard Doyle and J. R. Planché. London: George Routledge and Sons, 1868.

71. **Anderson, Anne.** *The Sleeping Beauty.* London: Thomas Nelson and Sons, Ltd., n.d.

72. **Doré, Gustave.** *Fairy Tales Told Again.* London: Cassell, Petter, and Galpin, n.d.

73. **Dulac, Edmund.** *The Sleeping Beauty and Other Fairy Tales.* Retold by Sir Arthur Quiller-Couch. New York: Hodder and Stoughton, n.d.

74. **Anonymous.** *The Ideal Fairy Tales,* n.d.

75. **Sowerby, Millicent.** *Grimm's Fairy Tales.* Retold by Githa Sowerby. London: Grant Richards, 1909.

76. **Anonymous.** *The Ideal Fairy Tales,* n.d.

77. **Rackham, Arthur.** *The Sleeping Beauty.* Retold by C. S. Evans. London: William Heinemann, 1920.

78. **Anonymous.** *The Ideal Fairy Tales,* n.d.

79. **Anonymous.** *The Favourite Book of Nursery Tales.* London: Thomas Nelson and Sons, 1893.

80. **Robinson, W. Heath.** *Old Time Stories,* by Charles Perrault, translated by A. E. Johnson. New York: Dodd, Mead and Co., 1921.

81. **Hassall, John.** *The Old Nursery Stories and Rhymes.* London: Blackie and Son, Ltd., n.d.

82. **Robinson, Charles.** *The Big Book of Fairy Tales.* Edited by Walter Jerrold. New York: H. M. Caldwell Co.; London: Blackie and Son, Ltd., n.d.

83. **Anonymous.** *My Nursery Tale Book.* New York: E. P. Dutton and Co.; London: Ernest Nister, n.d.

84. **Anonymous.** *The Favourite Book of Nursery Tales.* London: Thomas Nelson and Sons, 1893.

85. **Rackham, Arthur.** *The Fairy Tales of the Brothers Grimm.* Translated by Mrs. Edgar Lucas. London: Constable and Co. Ltd., 1909.

86. **Rackham, Arthur.** *The Fairy Tales of the Brothers Grimm.* Translated by Mrs. Edgar Lucas. London: Constable and Co. Ltd., 1909.

87. **Anonymous.** *Mother Goose Nursery Tales,* n.d.

88. **Folkard, Charles.** *Grimm's Fairy Tales.* London: Adam and Charles Black, 1911.

89. **Doré, Gustave.** *Fairy Tales Told Again.* London: Cassell, Petter, and Galpin, n.d.

90. **Anonymous.** *The Favourite Book of Nursery Tales.* London: Thomas Nelson and Sons, 1893.

91. **Harbour, Jennie.** *My Book of Favourite Fairy Tales.* Edited by Capt. Eric Vredenburg. London: Raphael Tuck and Sons, Ltd.; Philadelphia: David McKay Co., n.d.

92. **Gobel, Warwick.** *The Fairy Book.* London: Macmillan and Co., Ltd., 1913.

93. **Anonymous.** *Mother Goose Nursery Tales,* n.d.

94. **Newell, Peter.** *Favorite Fairy Tales.* New York: Harper and Brothers Publishers, 1907.

95. **Dulac, Edmund.** *The Sleeping Beauty and Other Fairy Tales.* Retold by Sir Arthur Quiller-Couch. New York: Hodder and Stoughton, n.d.

96. **Woodroffe, Paul.** *Nursery Tales,* by Amy Steedman. London: T. C. and E. C. Jack; New York: E. P. Dutton and Co., n.d.

97. **Smith, Jessie Willcox.** *A Child's Book of Stories.* Edited by Penrhyn W. Coussens. New York: Duffield and Co., 1919.

98. **Rackham, Arthur.** *The Arthur Rackham Fairy Book.* Edited by Arthur Rackham. Philadelphia: J. B. Lippincott Co., n.d.

99. **Anonymous.** *The Nursery Picture Book.* London: Raphael Tuck and Sons, Ltd., n.d.

100. **Anonymous.** *Briar Rose and Other Tales.* London: Blackie and Son, Ltd., 1897.

101. **Anonymous.** *The Ideal Fairy Tales,* n.d.

102. **Speed, Lancelot.** *Fairy Tale Plays and How to Act Them,* by Lady Bell. London: Longmans, Green and Co., 1913.

103. **Crane, Walter.** *Household Stories by the Brothers Grimm.* Translated by Lucy Crane. London: Macmillan and Co., 1886.

106. **Hassall, John.** *Popular Nursery Stories.* London: Blackie and Son, Ltd., n.d.

107. **Anonymous.** *The Favourite Book of Nursery Tales.* London: Thomas Nelson and Sons, 1893.

108. **Vogel, Herm.** *Kinder und Hausmärchen,* by Jacob and Wilhelm Grimm. Munich: Braun and Schneider, n.d.

109. **Speed, Lancelot.** *The Red Fairy Book.* Edited by Andrew Lang. London: Longmans, Green and Co., 1890.

110. **Fripp, Innes.** *The Old Fairy Tales.* New York: Sully and Kleinteich, n.d.

111. **Livings, Bess.** *Snow White and the Seven Dwarfs,* Jacob and Wilhelm Grimm. Chicago: Rand McNally and Co., n.d.

112. **Crane, Walter.** *Household Stories by the Brothers Grimm.* Translated by Lucy Crane. London: Macmillan and Co., 1886.

113. **Margetson, W. H.** *The Old Fairy Tales.* New York: Sully and Kleinteich, n.d.

114. **Anonymous.** *My Nursery Tale Book.* New York: E. P. Dutton and Co.; London: Ernest Nister, n.d.

115. **Harbour, Jennie.** *My Book of Favourite Fairy Tales.* Edited by Capt. Eric Vredenburg. London: Raphael Tuck and Sons, Ltd.; Philadelphia: David McKay Co., n.d.

116. **Hassall, John.** *Popular Nursery Stories.* London: Blackie and Son, Ltd., n.d.

117. **Anonymous.** *My Nursery Tale Book.* New York: E. P. Dutton and Co.; London: Ernest Nister, n.d.

118. **Drupsteen, W. C.** *Snowdrop.* Retold by G. Van Der Hoeven. London: W. S. Partridge and Co., n.d.

119. **Livings, Bess.** *Snow White and the Seven Dwarfs,* by Jacob and Wilhelm Grimm. Chicago: Rand McNally and Co., n.d.

120. **Rackham, Arthur.** *The Fairy Tales of the Brothers Grimm.* Translated by Mrs. Edgar Lucas. London: Constable and Co. Ltd., 1909.

121. TOP: **Hassall, John.** *Popular Nursery Stories.* London: Blackie and Son, Ltd., n.d.
BOTTOM: **Robinson, Charles.** *The Big Book of Fairy Tales.* Edited by Walter Jerrold. New York: H. M. Caldwell Co.; London: Blackie and Son, Ltd., n.d.

122. **Newell, Peter.** *Favorite Fairy Tales.* New York: Harper and Brothers Publishers, 1907.

123. **Tarrant, Margaret.** *Fairy Tales.* London: Ward, Lock and Co. Ltd., n.d.

124. **Kubel, O.** *German postcard,* n.d.

125. **Folkard, Charles.** *Grimm's Fairy Tales.* London: Adam and Charles Black, 1911.

126. **Sowerby, Millicent.** *Grimm's Fairy Tales.* Retold by Githa Sowerby. London: Grant Richards, 1909.

127. **Smith, Jessie Willcox.** *A Child's Book of Stories.* Edited by Penrhyn W. Coussens. New York: Duffield and Co., 1919.

128. **Anonymous.** *The Old Fairy Tales.* New York: Sully and Kleinteich, n.d.

129. **Goble, Warwick.** *The Fairy Book.* London: Macmillan and Co. Ltd., 1913.

130. **Menerheim, Paul.** *Kinder und Hausmärchen,* Jacob and Wilhelm Grimm. Gütersloh: C. Bertelsmann, 1895.

131. **Vogel, Herm.** *Kinder und Hausmärchen,* by Jacob and Wilhelm Grimm. Munich: Braun and Schneider, n.d.

132. **Pocock, Noel.** *Grimm's Fairy Tales.* London: Henry, Frowde and Hodder and Stoughton, 1913.

133. **Robinson, Charles.** *The Big Book of Fairy Tales.* Edited by Walter Jerrold. New York: H. M. Caldwell Co.; London: Blackie and Son, Ltd., n.d.

134. **Robinson, Charles.** *The Big Book of Fairy Tales.* Edited by

Walter Jerrold. New York: H. M. Caldwell Co.; London: Blackie and Son, Ltd., n.d.

135. **Livings, Bess.** *Snow White and the Seven Dwarfs,* by Jacob and Wilhelm Grimm. Chicago: Rand McNally and Co., n.d.

136. **Anonymous.** *My Nursery Tale Book.* New York: E. P. Dutton and Co.; London: Ernest Nister, n.d.

137. **Tarrant, Margaret.** *Fairy Tales.* London: Ward, Lock and Co. Ltd., n.d.

138. **Choate, Florence.** *Stokes' Wonder Book of Fairy Tales.* Edited by Elisabeth Vernon Quinn. New York: Frederick A. Stokes Co., 1917.

139. **Falls, Charles.** *Snow White and the Seven Dwarfs,* by Jessie Braham White. New York: Dodd, Mead and Co., 1913.

140. **Rackham, Arthur.** *The Fairy Tales of the Brothers Grimm.* Translated by Mrs. Edgar Lucas. London: Constable and Co. Ltd., 1909.

141. **Livings, Bess.** *Snow White and the Seven Dwarfs,* by Jacob and Wilhelm Grimm. Chicago: Rand McNally and Co., n.d.

142. **Robinson, Charles.** *The Big Book of Fairy Tales.* Edited by Walter Jerrold. New York: H. M. Caldwell Co.; London: Blackie and Son, Ltd., n.d.

143. **Harbour, Jennie.** *My Book of Favourite Fairy Tales.* Edited by Capt. Eric Vredenburg. London: Raphael Tuck and Sons, Ltd.; Philadelphia: David McKay Co., n.d.

144. **Robinson, Charles.** *The Big Book of Fairy Tales.* Edited by Walter Jerrold. New York: H. M. Caldwell Co.; London: Blackie and Son, Ltd., n.d.

145. **Falls, Charles.** *Snow White and the Seven Dwarfs,* by Jessie Braham White. New York: Dodd, Mead and Co., 1913.

146. **Crane, Walter.** *Household Stories by the Brothers Grimm.* Translated by Lucy Crane. London: Macmillan and Co., 1886.

147. **Harbour, Jennie.** *My Book of Favourite Fairy Tales.* Edited by Capt. Eric Vredenburg. London: Raphael Tuck and Sons, Ltd.; Philadelphia: David McKay Co., n.d.

148. **Watson, A. H.** *Told Again,* by Walter de la Mare. New York: Alfred A. Knopf, 1927.

149. TOP: **Sowerby, Millicent.** *Grimm's Fairy Tales.* Retold by Githa Sowerby. London: Grant Richards, 1909.
BOTTOM: **Anonymous.** *My Nursery Tale Book.* New York: E. P. Dutton. London: Ernest Nister, n.d.

150. **Rackham, Arthur.** *The Fairy Tales of the Brothers Grimm.* Translated by Mrs. Edgar Lucas. London: Constable and Co. Ltd., 1909.

151. **Hassall, John.** *Popular Nursery Stories.* London: Blackie and

Son, Ltd., n.d.

152.   **Kubel, O.** *German postcard*, n.d.

153.   **Nielsen, Kay.** *Hansel and Gretel*, Jacob and Wilhelm Grimm. London: Hodder and Stoughton, 1925.

154.   **Speed, Lancelot.** *The Red Fairy Book.* Edited by Andrew Lang. London: Longmans, Green and Co., 1890.

155.   **Vogel, Herm.** *Kinder und Hausmärchen*, by Jacob and Wilhelm Grimm. Munich: Braun and Schneider, n.d.

156.   **Anonymous.** *Little Snow White.* London: George Routledge and Sons, c. 1870.

157.   **Anonymous.** *Ephemera.* n.d.

158.   **Godwin, Frank.** *Stories the Balloonman Told*, n.d.

159.   **Livings, Bess.** *Snow White and the Seven Dwarfs*, by Jacob and Wilhelm Grimm. Chicago: Rand McNally and Co., n.d.

160.   **Drupsteen, W. C.** *Snowdrop.* Retold by G. Van Der Hoeven. London: S. W. Partridge and Co., n.d.

161.   **Hassall, John.** *Popular Nursery Stories.* London: Blackie and Son, Ltd., n.d.

162.   **Drupsteen, W. C.** *Snowdrop.* Retold by G. Van Der Hoeven. London: S. W. Partridge and Co., n.d.

163.   **Speed, Lancelot.** *The Red Fairy Book.* Edited by Andrew Lang. London: Longmans, Green and Co., 1890.

164.   **Rackham, Arthur.** *Cinderella.* Retold by C. S. Evans. London: William Heinemann; Philadelphia: J. B. Lippincott Co., 1919.

165.   **Nielsen, Kay.** *Hansel and Gretel*, by Jacob and Wilhelm Grimm. London: Hodder and Stoughton, 1925.

166.   **Anonymous.** *The Favourite Book of Nursery Tales.* London: Thomas Nelson and Sons, 1893.

167.   **Drupsteen, W. C.** *Snowdrop.* Retold by G. Van Der Hoeven. London: S. W. Partridge and Co., n.d.

172.   **Crane, Walter.** *Household Stories by the Brothers Grimm.* Translated by Lucy Crane. London: Macmillan and Co., 1886

Back cover: LEFT. **Gunston, W.** *Cinderella.* London: Frederick Warne and Co., c. 1876.

CENTER. **Sowerby, Millicent.** *Grimm's Fairy Tales.* Retold by Githa Sowerby. London: Grant Richards, 1909.

RIGHT. **Anonymous.** *My Nursery Tale Book.* New York: E. P. Dutton and Co.; London: Ernest Nister, n.d.